HarperAlley is an imprint of HarperCollins Publishers.

FGTeeV: GAME BREAK!

ISBN 978-0-06-309298-3

Typography by Jessica Nordskog and Erica De Chavez
21 22 23 24 25   PC/WOR   10 9 8 7 6 5 4 3 2 1
❖
First Edition

Are you reading the copyright page?! You must be a real FGTeeV fan! True fans get a bonus activity. Hidden throughout the book are eleven teeny-tiny gurkey turkeys for you to find. Good luck!

WHAT ELSE SHOULD THEY HAVE FOR BREAKFAST?

```
P Q V B S Y Z R G P R X N W
W A D J G B P J O K Y O O A
G W N Q G M N A F H C M X F
D N X C E K T L O A N X H F
H U Y L A M V W B Q W X I L
H B C O E K K Y Q Y M L F E
M O R A N G E J U I C E O S
J X L Z M K A S O V B B V N
V L W W R L S B Z E Y J W J
E K S U U B P V U F S Z B P
L M T S O G G Z D P H B O J
E F Z P B L A E R E C Z P L
```

TURKEY BACON   EGGS   CEREAL   OATMEAL
ORANGE JUICE   WAFFLES   PANCAKES   BAGEL

WHAT FOODS SHOULDN'T BE ON THE MENU?
Unscramble the words to find out!

yumgm rabes _____ _____

eheces labsl _____ _____

oht ucsea _hot_ _sauce_

kiplcse _____

The FGTeeV family loves nicknames. Add either **STER**, **O**, **Y**, or **Z** to the names below to make a nickname.

DUDD_Y_

LEX_O_

MIKE_ _ _ _

MOOM_Y_

CONNECT THE DOTS TO SEE DUDDY.

5

abandoned   dark

cozy   frightening

peaceful   normal   pretty

terrifying

SPOOKADILLY MANOR IS FILLED WITH GHOSTS.

Flip a coin to escape the haunted stairways.

Heads = move two spaces forward

Tails = move one space forward

Follow the instructions on the stair where you land. If it's blank, flip the coin again. Try to reach the finish line in as few coin flips as possible.

START

MOVE FORWARD ONE

MOVE BACK ONE

BWAHAHAHA!!

END

MOVE UP ONE

How many flips
did it take?

_____

MOVE BACK TWO

9

OH NO, YOU'RE TRAPPED IN A DEAD END! COMPLETE THE WORD LADDER TO CLIMB OUT.

Write a word that begins with an "a" on the first rung. On the second rung, write a word that begins with the second letter of your first word. And on the third rung, write a word that begins with the second letter of your second word, and so on until you reach the top.

You're free!

Try not to use two words that begin with the same letter!

a _____

DANCE BREAK!

BEEN GAMING TOO LONG? JUMP UP AND BOOGIE DOWN FOR 15 SECONDS. SHOW OFF YOUR BEST MOVES!

Forget the ladder, I would fight my way out!

Using the clues below, insert words into the blank spaces to see how Lexi would escape the dead end.

1. **Adjective**

2. **Body part**

3. **Piece of furniture**

4. **Noun**

5. **Name of a game**

I pick up my (1) _____ axe,

swing it over my (2)_____,

and bring it crashing down on the

(3)_____. We burst

through the (4)_____ and

run out of (5) _____.

When I went to bed, Duddy was still playing. He wanted to use his sword to slice ghosts like a samurai.

FINISH THE CROSSWORD TO FIND OTHER WEAPONS HE COULD USE TO BATTLE GHOSTS.

ACROSS

1. Pointed tipped weapon with a long shaft you can thrust or throw
2. Huge gun that shoots explosive shells
3. Small bomb you throw

DOWN

3. Shoots bullets
4. Tool with handle and sharp steel blade
5. Sharp blade on a handle
6. Explosive device

Maybe Duddz is out walking Oreo?

Which one is Oreo? She's one of the eight dogs shown that looks different. Circle her when you spot her!

JOKE TIME!
What's black and white, black and white, and black and white?

For answer, see page 121

What if Oreo got off her leash? Duddy might be trying to catch her.

Help Oreo get to Duddy by drawing a line from each math problem to its correct answer.

Draw where you think Oreo could have gone.

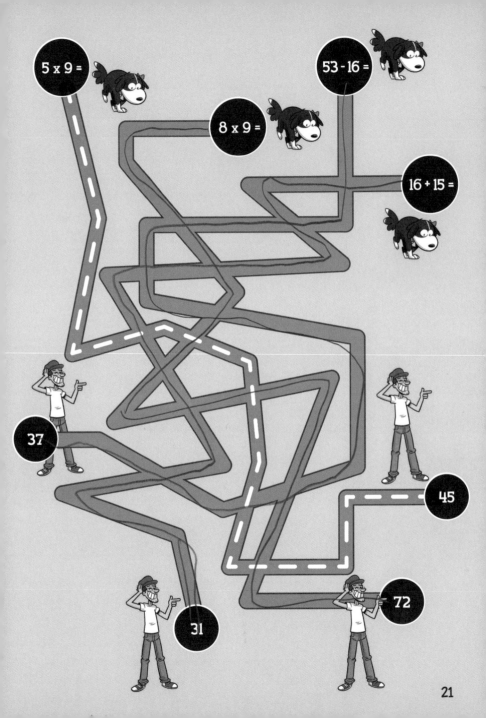

23

WHAT DOES SHAWN
SAY TO OREO WHEN HE
GIVES HER A TREAT?
USE THE KEY BELOW
TO FIGURE IT OUT.

A = Z	N = M
B = y	O = L
C = X	P = K
D = W	Q = J
E = V	R = I
F = U	S = H
G = T	T = G
H = S	U = F
I = R	V = E
J = Q	W = D
K = P	X = C
L = O	y = B
M = N	Z = A

Well, Duddster isn't with Oreo. Maybe he's playing Diaper Drop against that jerk Big Baby.

Draw Big Baby's bottom half— don't forget the stinky diaper!

Big Baby's diaper isn't just stinky. Find and circle the words in the smelly search below.

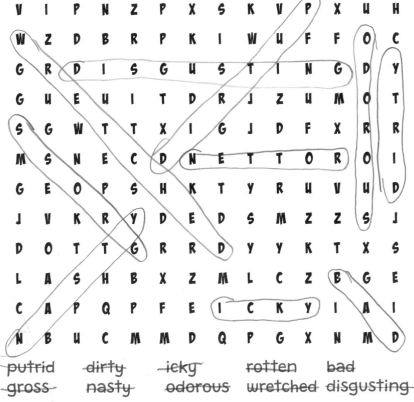

V I P N Z P X S K V P X U H
W Z D B R P K I W U F F O C
G R D I S G U S T I N G D Y
G U E U I T D R J Z U M O T
S G W T T X I G J D F X R R
M S N E C D N E T T O R O I
G E O P S H K T Y R U V U D
J V K R Y D E D S M Z Z S J
D O T T G R R D Y Y K T X S
L A S H B X Z M L C Z B G E
C A P Q P F E I C K Y I A I
N B U C M M D Q P G X N M D

putrid   dirty   icky   rotten   bad
gross   nasty   odorous   wretched disgusting

IN *DIAPER DROP*, YOU HAVE TO CLIMB A BUILDING TO SAVE BIG BABY.

Draw a line through the numbers with the greatest value on the scaffolding to get to the top.

BEEN GAMING TOO LONG? JUMP UP AND BOOGIE DOWN FOR 15 SECONDS. SHOW OFF YOUR BEST MOVES!

DANCE BREAK!

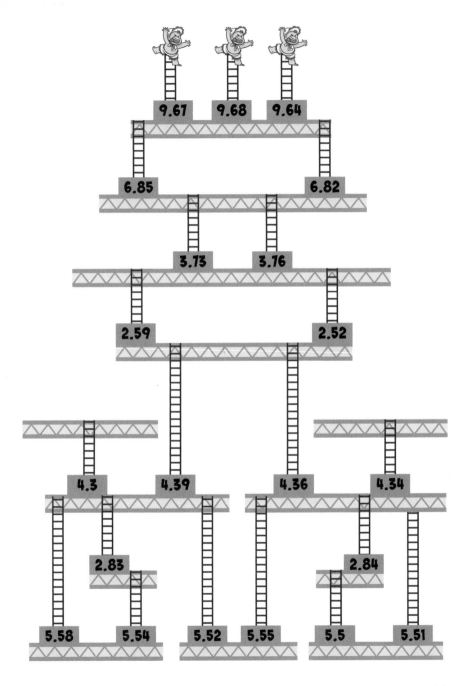

BIG BABY TRIES TO KNOCK YOU OFF THE BUILDING BY HITTING YOU WITH HIS POOP-FILLED DIAPER.

Circle what you'd rather be hit with than a stinky diaper:

pail of slop   box of rocks

basket of hissing vipers

rotten eggs

feather pillow

Then draw a line to connect the
missile and the name of a villain
who would throw it at you:

box of rocks

hissing vipers

feather pillow

pail of slop

rotten eggs

Sooey Pig

Caveman Carl

Lord Snake Pit

Cluck Cluck Buck

Super Soft Sally

Using the clues below, insert words into the blank spaces to see how Mike would defeat Big Baby.

1. Adjective
2. Noun
3. Something stinky
4. Favorite bad guy
5. Something tall

Mike climbs the (1) _____ building,

holding tight to the (2) _____ .

When Big Baby lets go with a giant

(3) _____ , Mike catches it.

He whips it back at (4) _____

_____ , knocking him from the

(5) _____ .

Duddy wears a shirt with the FGTeeV logo.

Mike's shirt has a cool design made out of his name.

CREATE A LOGO FOR
YOUR NAME ON THE T-SHIRT
ON THE FACING PAGE.

Let's play Super-Realistic Zombie Battles from the War of 1812.

Duddy loved the game when he was a kid.

Figure out the clues to fill in this CORPSE-FILLED crossword.

ACROSS

1. Dark time of day
2. Undead creature
4. What zombies eat

DOWN

3. When the dead suddenly rise and eat the living
5. What zombie mouths would do to your brains
6. Corpses that come back to life

DUDDY'S FAVORITE CHARACTER WHEN HE WAS A KID WAS COLONEL CORN.

On the facing page, draw a hero who would be good at fighting zombies.

Create a name for your zombie hunter using words from the word bank.

BURNING

DOCTOR

MASTER

INSANE

PLAGUE

HEADSHOT

TERROR

HEAVY

FIRE

EVIL

WARRIOR

FURY

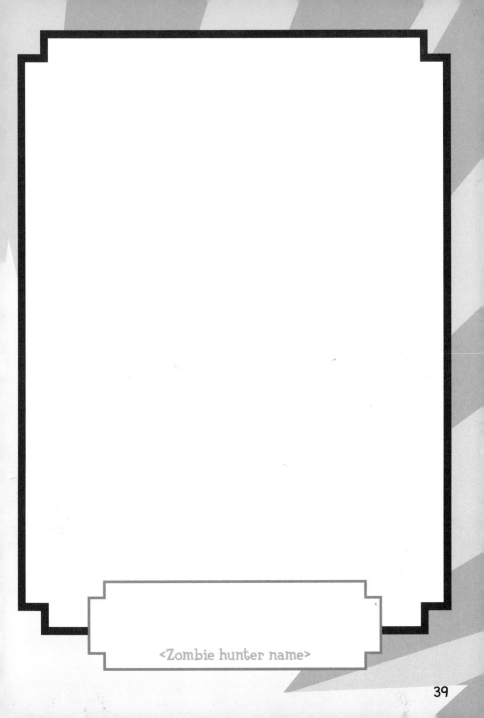

<Zombie hunter name>

Compare the avatars on the left to the avatars on the right. Can you find all ten differences?

What's a ghost's favorite game?

Use the key below to find the answer.

1 = E	6 = A
2 = I	7 = K
3 = D	8 = N
4 = S	9 = R
5 = H	

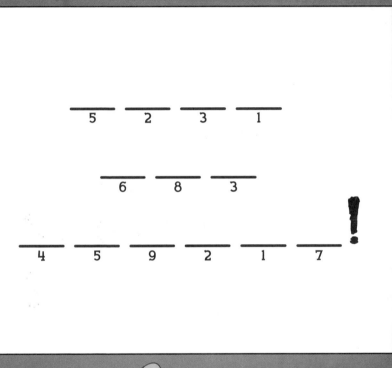

$$\overline{5} \quad \overline{2} \quad \overline{3} \quad \overline{1}$$

$$\overline{6} \quad \overline{8} \quad \overline{3}$$

$$\overline{4} \quad \overline{5} \quad \overline{9} \quad \overline{2} \quad \overline{1} \quad \overline{7} \quad !$$

DANCE BREAK!

BEEN GAMING TOO LONG? JUMP UP AND BOOGIE DOWN FOR 15 SECONDS. SHOW OFF YOUR BEST MOVES!

IN *ZOMBIE BATTLES*, THE MILITIA MUST ESCAPE THE ZOMBIES.

Flip a coin to help them get away.

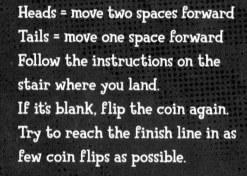

Start

Heads = move two spaces forward
Tails = move one space forward
Follow the instructions on the stair where you land.
If it's blank, flip the coin again.
Try to reach the finish line in as few coin flips as possible.

Move back one

Move forward two

Move back one

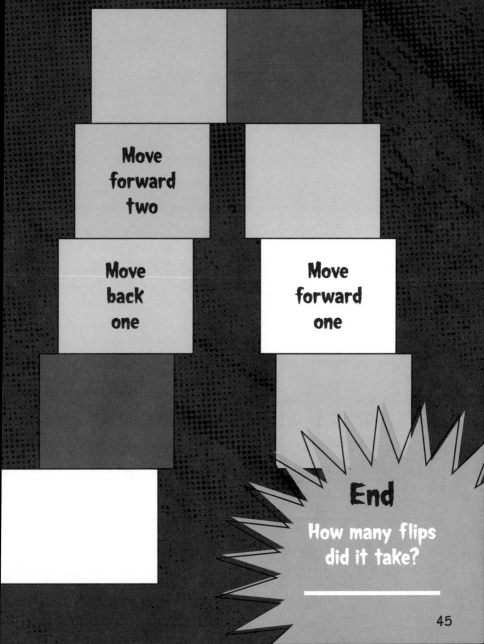

Move
forward
two

Move
back
one

Move
forward
one

End

How many flips
did it take?

IT'S NOT EASY TO GET AWAY.
MIKE HAS TO TRY A BUNCH
OF DIFFERENT ROUTES.

START

END

START

END

Hey, Shawn, let me play.

CHASE, MIKE, AND SHAWN MAKE A GREAT TEAM AGAINST THE ZOMBIES.

WHAT POWERS HELP THEM GET AWAY?
FIND THE WORDS BELOW IN THE SEARCH
ON THE NEXT PAGE.

run   shoot   escape
jump   clone   battle
hide   power up   kick
punch   hop   blast

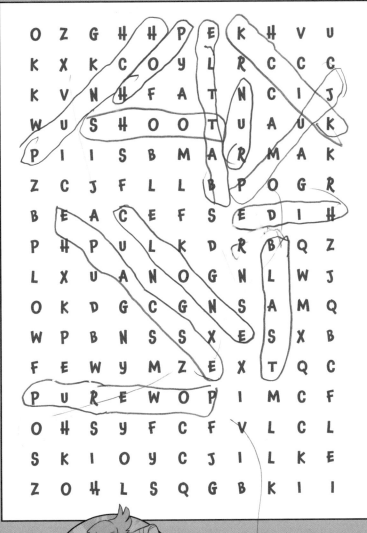

Swap the letters for some ideas.

1 = A   10 = J   19 = S

2 = B   11 = K   20 = T

3 = C   12 = L   21 = U

4 = D   13 = M   22 = V

5 = E   14 = N   23 = W

6 = F   15 = O   24 = X

7 = G   16 = P   25 = Y

8 = H   17 = Q   26 = Z

9 = I   18 = R

Oh my goodness,

He's right ——— me.

He's gonna ——— me.

I've gotta ———.

This ain't no ———.

Boom bash ———

I've gotta ———.

53

Yeah, but he's never going to beat his game-filled rap on gurkey turkey.

Don't recognize the word **"GURKEY"**? That's because it is a word Duddy made up that means **SCARED**. So if you are a **GURKEY TURKEY**, it means you are easily frightened.

Create ten words (or more!) from the phrase "I'M A GURKEY TURKEY"

_____

_____

_____

_____

_____

_____

_____

_____

_____

_____

EVEN THOUGH DUDDY'S RHYMES ARE TIGHT, HE'S NOT A GREAT SPELLER.

Circle the five misspelled words in the rap below:

Hey-yo, Pops, want to playe this game?

No thanks, kid, that looks lame.

No, I promese, it's really cool!

Yeah right, it looks old skool.

No! Try it, you mite like it!

All right, don't get so exsited.

DANCE BREAK!

BEEN GAMING TOO LONG? JUMP UP AND BOOGIE DOWN FOR 15 SECONDS. SHOW OFF YOUR BEST MOVES!

Duddy is probably at the game store, looking for classics.

Draw a scene from your favorite old-school video game.

Draw a line from Duddy through as many cheese balls as you can without running into Oreo.

The most you can get is

──────── .

WHAT WOULD YOU EAT?

Find and circle the FGTeeV fam favorites in the word search on the facing page.

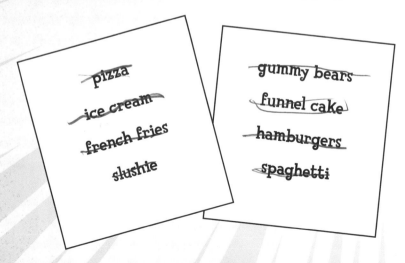

pizza

ice cream

french fries

slushie

gummy bears

funnel cake

hamburgers

spaghetti

I	H	K	L	F	X	S	T	X	O	A	S
C	L	H	C	R	Q	L	L	D	C	Q	R
E	B	C	U	E	V	J	A	T	G	N	E
C	Q	T	R	N	C	H	W	M	P	G	G
R	E	K	A	C	L	E	N	N	U	F	R
E	P	V	I	H	Y	E	C	M	B	I	U
A	O	P	X	F	P	V	M	X	T	D	B
M	E	C	W	R	K	Y	D	T	X	C	M
T	Z	Y	S	I	B	C	E	Q	F	I	A
B	L	V	P	E	I	H	T	W	X	H	H
P	R	Y	A	S	G	J	Z	K	O	H	I
O	I	R	B	A	J	N	R	R	U	W	I
W	S	Z	P	S	L	U	S	H	I	E	X
P	D	S	Z	X	V	C	D	Q	R	L	M
R	O	A	I	A	Q	K	M	Y	T	J	B

I'd much rather buy some new clothes.

Circle the pants Lexi would want.
Hint: the ones not covered in condiments!

How much money does Lexi have to spend on pants?

This is what she has in her wallet:

two $5 bills	seven $1 bills

one $10 bill

four quarters

eight dimes

Total:

$ __ __ . __ __

I'd just hang out with the old people.

OLD PEOPLE LOVE SHAWN BECAUSE HE IS SO CUTE.

Circle words old people might use to describe Shawn.

darling

rotten

precious

**Complete the number patterns
to get Moomy out of the mall:**

5, ___, 21, 29, ___, 45

1, 3, 9, 27, ___

22, 29, ___, 43, ___

16, 13, ___, 7, ___

___, 4, 8, 16, ___

Help Duddy get out of the mall by filling in the empty squares with one of the missing numbers (1–6) or the missing icons (■, ●, ★).

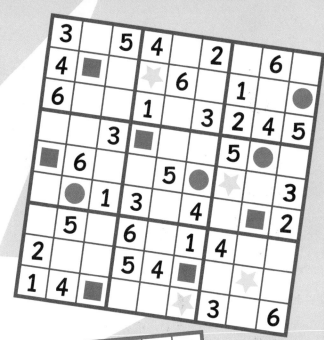

But be sure to use each of them just once in each row and in each column.

Cecil is the worst to game with because he freaks out if he loses. Use the numbers below to figure out Duddy's excuse for not having him over.

E = 5   I = 13

M = 9   F = 1

A = 7   S = 15

G = 3   L = 17

T = 11   Y = 19

WHAT DO ALL THE NUMBER CLUES HAVE IN COMMON?

For answer, see page 125

$$\overline{}_{3} \quad \overline{}_{7} \quad \overline{}_{9} \quad \overline{}_{5}$$

$$\overline{}_{11} \quad \overline{}_{13} \quad \overline{}_{9} \quad \overline{}_{5} \qquad \overline{}_{13} \quad \overline{}_{15}$$

$$\overline{}_{1} \quad \overline{}_{7} \quad \overline{}_{9} \quad \overline{}_{13} \quad \overline{}_{17} \quad \overline{}_{19}$$

$$\overline{}_{11} \quad \overline{}_{13} \quad \overline{}_{9} \quad \overline{}_{5}$$

DANCE BREAK!

BEEN GAMING TOO LONG? JUMP UP AND BOOGIE DOWN FOR 15 SECONDS. SHOW OFF YOUR BEST MOVES!

Create a list of ten critters, the first starting with the letter C. On the second line, write the name of a critter that begins with the second letter of your first word. And on the third line, write the name of a critter that begins with the second letter of your second word, and so on until you've filled in all ten.

C _____

_____

_____

_____

_____

_____

_____

_____

_____

_____

THE GOAL OF *CRITTER CRAVINGS* IS TO SAVE FRANKLIN'S LAND FROM INVADING ANIMALS.

Flip a coin to get relish weapons you'll need to fight them off.

Heads = move two spaces forward
Tails = move one space forward

Follow the instructions on the spot where you land.

If it's blank, flip the coin again.

Try to reach the finish line in as few coin flips as possible.

START

MOVE AHEAD ONE

Why relish? Who knows!

How many flips
did it take?

_____

IN THE FIRST LEVEL OF *CRITTER CRAVINGS*, PLAYERS FIGHT OFF KILLER PRAIRIE DOGS.

Find and circle the one prairie dog that seems friendly.

Prairie dogs live together in colonies in burrows underground. Draw an underground home for killer prairie dogs.

IN THE FINAL LEVEL OF *CRITTER CRAVINGS,* PLAYERS HAVE TO DEFEAT THE BIG BOSS.

Connect the dots to reveal the creature.

Unscramble the letters below to reveal other weapon sounds!

ambl   _____

gbna   _____

owp   _____

ahwm   _____

oo-abkm   _____

rccak   _____

Get back, you _____

I'll be that _____

I'll aim to stop _____

All up in your side,
my bullets they _____

I be down with the _____

Tell me, is you down _____?

COPPER
PEW
YOU

ROBBER
TOO
GOT YOU

DUDDY LOVES FUNNY EXPRESSIONS.

DANCE BREAK!

BEEN GAMING TOO LONG? JUMP UP AND BOOGIE DOWN FOR 15 SECONDS. SHOW OFF YOUR BEST MOVES!

Connect each expression
with a line to its meaning.

Peace out

Oh snap!

Hater

Cha-ching

Boom

Fired up

Up on my back

Homies

Behind me

I got you

Friends

You've been insulted

I'm excited

Just made money

Goodbye

Someone who is jealous

Starting with the word **sleep**, draw a line that passes through the fish with words that change only one letter each time to make a new word, ending on the word **dream**. The first one has been done for you.

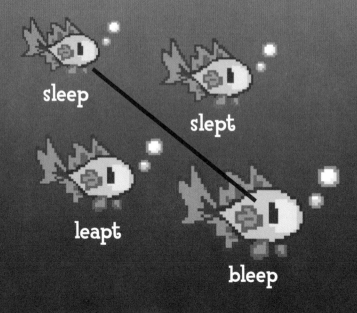

sleep

slept

leapt

bleep

dress

dream

dread

broom

board

bread

depth

bleak

bleed

bleep

breed

BESIDES FEEDING YOUR FISH
AND CHANGING ITS GRAVEL
COLOR, THERE'S NOT MUCH
TO DO IN THE GAME.

Fill in the letters next to the images to
show what you can't do with your fish.

w _ _ _

p _ _ _

p _ _

THE FISH JUST SWIMS SLOWLY AROUND. THAT'S WHY DUDDY RENAMED THE GAME *MY BORING PET FISH*.

FUN FACT: Duddy is color blind, which means he can't easily tell the difference between red and green. He'd have trouble finding the difference if the fish were those colors.

Can you find and circle the one fish in the tank that isn't bored?

If you were to create a more interesting fish, what would it look like?

DRAW IT HERE.

Name your new fish, picking one word from the first column and one from the second.

Captain	Bubbles
Mighty	Squirt
Big	Moby
Tiny	Goldie
Doctor	Coral
Mister	Blue
Lucky	Finn

New fish name

MOOMY DIDN'T MEAN TO CREATE A TERRIFYING VILLAIN FOR HER GAME.

WHAT WOULD YOU DO IF YOU WERE TRAPPED IN AN AQUARIUM?

Flip a coin to escape.

Heads = move two spaces forward

Tails = move one space forward

Follow the instructions on the spot where you land.

If it's blank, flip the coin again.

Try to escape in as few coin flips as possible.

START

Swim forward one

Swin backwa thre

Swim
backward
one

Swim
forward
one

Swim
backward
one

YOU
ESCAPED!

Swim
forward
two

HOW MANY FLIPS DID IT TAKE?

KRASH!

DOOM

If I were trapped in an aquarium, I'd use an axe to break out.

It's your turn to be the writer! Fill in the word balloons with what Moomy and Duddy would say as they try to escape the crazy fish and king crab.

Is your answer greater (>)
or less (<) than
480?

_____

-2

+18

-14

+22

-7

+14

Start with
the number **444**

Starting with the word **SHIP**, create a ladder to escape the submarine using the clues to reach the **NAVY**.

NAVY

take away
a letter and
change vowels

armed forces at sea

take away
a letter and
change one

a fiction book

add a letter
to the end

a digging tool

change
one letter

to push

change
one letter

remove hair from face

change
one letter

the form of something

add two
letters

a guilty feeling

change
one letter

a meat served with eggs

change
one letter

male pronoun

delete
one letter

a body part

SHIP

starting word

Or maybe Duddy is playing a boxing game?

Find the answer to each problem on the right. Then look at the key below to find the letter that corresponds to each answer. The phrase revealed will be the sound of Duddy getting punched.

W = 213

O = 145

P = 265

C = 99

U = 278

H = 58

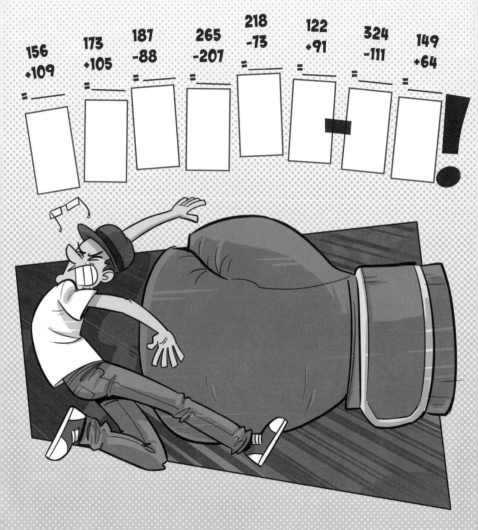

Use shapes from the shape bank on the next page to draw your own city.

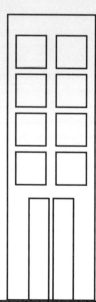

SHAPE BANK

CIRCLE WHAT DUDDY WOULD NEED TO PLAY A GAME.

Design the ultimate controller for your game,
assigning a command for each button.

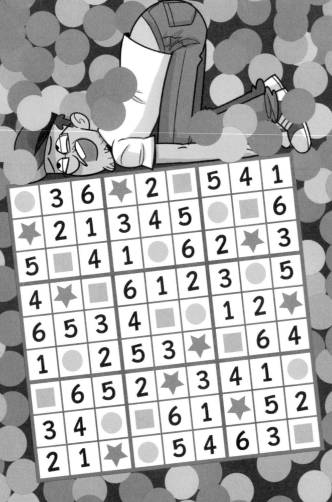

Help him get out by filling in the empty squares with the numbers 1–6 and shapes.

But be sure to use each of them just once in each row and in each column.

While I was asleep, I had the weirdest dream about being a mermaid. I was on the seafood diet.

What's the seafood diet?

Use the key below to find the answer.

A = Z   J = Q   S = H
B = Y   K = P   T = G
C = X   L = O   U = F
D = W   M = N   V = E
E = V   N = M   W = D
F = U   O = L   X = C
G = T   P = K   Y = B
H = S   Q = J   Z = A
I = R   R = I

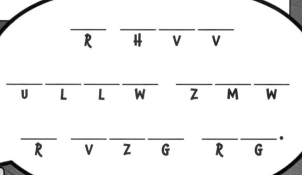

_R_ _H_ _V_ _V_

_U_ _L_ _L_ _W_   _Z_ _M_ _W_

_R_ _V_ _Z_ _G_ _R_ _G_ .

115

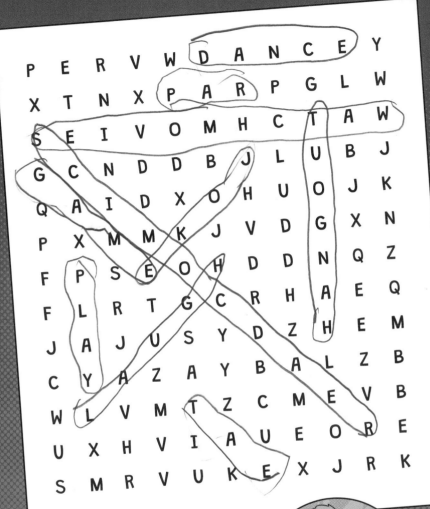

ACROSS

1. Favorite of old people
2. Kid boss
3. Middle boy
4. Frightened fowl
5. OB (oldest boy)
6. Fun-loving rapper
7. Best dog ever

DOWN

6. Rap about laser gun sound
8. Woman in charge

HOW WELL DO YOU NOW KNOW THE FGTEEV FAMILY? FILL IN THE CROSSWORD BELOW AND SEE.

ANSWER KEY

Page 2

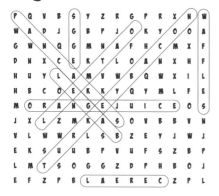

Page 3

gummy bears
cheese balls
hot sauce
pickles

Page 4

Duddy
Lexo
Mikester
Moomz

Page 5

Page 6

welcoming
safe
friendly
cozy
peaceful
normal
pretty

Page 11

Page 17

					K		B	
			C	A	N	N	O	N
S	P	E	A	R			I		M	
			X			F		B
	G	R	E	N	A	D	E	
	U						
	N						

Page 19

Answer to joke:
Oreo rolling down a hill.

Page 21

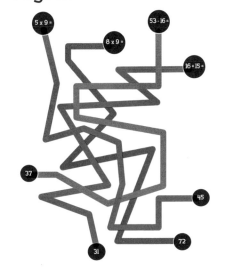

Pages 22–23

line, fine, five, dive, live, like, lake, cake, cape, tape

Page 25

Who's a good girl?

Page 27

Page 29

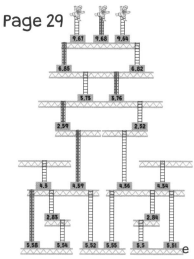

Page 31

box of rocks — Sooey Pig
hissing vipers — Caveman Carl
feather pillow — Lord Snake Pit
pail of slop — Cluck Cluck Buck
rotten eggs — Super Soft Sally

Page 37

						U	
	B	R	A	I	N	S	
						D	
	Z	O	M	B	I	E	
	U			I		A	
N	I	G	H	T		D	
	T			E			
	B						
	R						
	E						
	A						
	K						

Pages 40–41

Page 43
Hide and Shriek!

Page 46

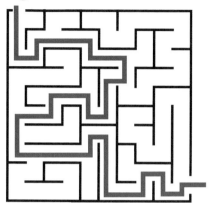

Page 47

Page 49

Page 51
transforming
fighting
chilling

Page 53
He's right **behind** me.
He's gonna **find** me.
I've gotta **run**.
This ain't no **fun**.
Boom bash **crash**
I've gotta **dash**.

Page 57

playe = play
promese = promise
skool = school
mite = might
exsited = excited

Page 59

The most you can get is 12.

Page 61

Page 62

Page 63

$28.80

Pages 64–65

darling
precious
adorable
dear

Page 67

5, 13, 21, 29, 37, 45
1, 3, 9, 27, 81
22, 29, 36, 43, 50
16, 13, 10, 7, 4
2, 4, 8, 16, 32

Page 69

Left grid:

3	1	5	4	●	2	■	6	★
4	■	2	★	6	5	1	3	●
6	★	●	1	■	3	2	4	5
★	2	3	■	1	6	5	●	4
■	6	4	2	5	●	★	1	3
5	●	1	3	★	4	6	■	2
●	5	★	6	3	1	4	2	■
2	3	6	5	4	■	●	★	1
1	4	■	●	2	★	3	5	6

Right grid:

4	3	■	2	6	★	●	1	5
6	●	★	4	5	1	2	3	■
1	5	2	■	3	●	★	4	6
●	■	4	3	1	2	6	5	★
★	1	5	6	4	■	3	●	2
3	2	6	★	●	5	1	■	4
5	★	3	●	■	6	4	2	1
2	4	1	5	★	3	■	6	●
■	6	●	1	2	4	5	★	3

Page 70

They are all
odd numbers.

Page 71

Game time is
family time

Page 78

Page 81

Page 83

blam
bang
pow
wham
ka–boom
crack

Page 85

robber
copper
you
got you
pew
too

Page 87

Peace out = Goodbye

Oh snap! = You've been insulted

Hater = Someone who is jealous

Cha-ching = Just made money

Boom = I got you

Fired up = I'm excited

Up on my back = Behind me

Homies = Friends

Pages 88-89

sleep, bleep, bleed, breed, bread, dread, dream.

Pages 90-91

walk
play
pet

Page 93

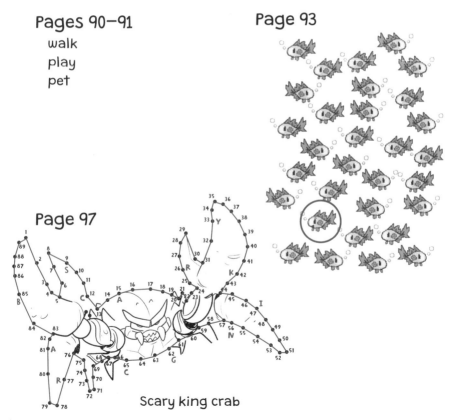

Page 97

Scary king crab

Page 103

LESS THAN 480

-2   475
+18   477
-14   459
+22   473
-7   451
+14   458

Page 105

ship, hip, him, ham,
shame, shape, shave,
shove, shovel, novel, navy

Page 107

PUCHOW-WW!

Pages 110–111

Page 113

●	6	4	2	3	5	■	★	1
■	5	1	●	★	6	2	4	3
★	2	3	■	4	1	6	●	5
4	●	6	★	5	2	1	3	■
3	■	2	1	●	4	★	5	6
5	1	★	6	■	3	●	2	4
6	★	5	4	1	●		■	2
2	3	■	5	6	★	4	1	●
1	4	●	3	2	■	5	6	★

3	6	5	■	●	★	2	4	1
●	4	★	2	1	6	3	■	5
2	■	1	5	4	3	★	●	6
4	5	6	★	2	●	1	3	■
■	★	●	3	6	1	4	5	2
1	3	2	4	■	5	6	★	●
★	1	3	●	5	2	■	6	4
6	●	4	1	3	■	5	2	★
5	2	■	6	★	4	●	1	3

Page 115

I see food and I eat it.

Page 117

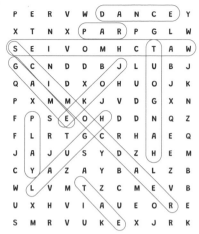

Page 119

Bonus Activity: The eleven gurkey turkeys are on pages 15, 23, 31, 70, 77, 78, 86, 92, 104, 114, and 118.